The
Treasure chest

Also in this series

The Rescue of Maid Marian (1)
The Silver Arrow (3)

YOUNG ROBIN HOOD
and
THE
TREASURE CHEST

RICHARD PERCY

MADCAP

To Mum
With love

First published in Great Britain in 1999
by Madcap Books,
André Deutsch Ltd,
76 Dean Street,
London, W1V 5HA

www.vci.co.uk

A catalogue record for this title is available from the
British Library

ISBN 0 233 99515 3

Typeset by Derek Doyle & Associates,
Mold, Flintshire
Printed by Mackays of Chatham plc

contents

Treetop Rescue

1

'Robin! Wake up! We need your help!' Someone was shaking him roughly. Robin looked sleepily at Marian's worried face. He sat up, rubbing his eyes.

'What's wrong?' He was instantly alert. After all, he had overall responsibility for the thirty children hidden in the secret camp of Sherwood Forest. He and his five committee members.

'It's little Mary,' said Marian. 'She's stuck up a tree.'

Inwardly, Robin felt relief. At least it wasn't an outside danger. He and his band were in hiding from the evil Sheriff of Nottingham and his men. Four weeks ago the men from their village of Edwinstowe had left on a mission to rescue good King Richard from imprisonment in Vienna. He would only be released if they could gather one thousand gold sovereigns for his ransom, otherwise the men themselves would be taken as slaves.

Robin jumped up and followed Marian to the other side of the clearing. The rest of the children were gathered under the elm tree which had quickly become a favourite for the younger children to play on. It had many branches around its trunk, making it easy to climb.

No one, however, had ever been as far up the tree as poor little four-year-old Mary was now. What's more, she had found her way to the end of one of the thin branches towards the top of the tree.

'Why on earth did she go all the way up there?' asked Robin. He watched with a sinking heart as even Mary's small body was making the branch bend horribly.

It was William, the cheeky ten-year-old, who answered.

'She was chasing her favourite squirrel. When he ran up the tree she followed. That branch is so thin that we daren't follow.'

Robin could see exactly what William meant. There was no way it would be safe for anyone capable of saving her to reach her. And the thin branch she was on was bending so much that even she could not climb back along it.

'Don't move, Mary!' shouted Robin. 'Hold on tight. We'll soon have you down.'

He sounded more confident than he felt and Mary's only answer was to wail even louder. Poor little child, he thought. She was in a very dangerous position and at the moment he couldn't think how he was going to rescue her. For the first time in the four weeks since they had come to the camp, Robin felt scared by the responsibility that he had taken on.

He turned to Little John and Michael, who stood beside him.

'What are we going to do?' He kept his voice low so that the other children could not hear the panic in his voice.

'Could you not fix a rope to an arrow and then fire it into the branch beside her?' asked Little John, for Robin Hood was well-known for his archery. 'Little Mary could then tie the rope round herself and we could lower her down.'

There were murmurs of disagreement from the three young women who stood nearby.

'You can't do that,' said Anna, who was in

5

charge of the young ones since she had had much experience as the eldest of her family. The poor little thing doesn't know how to tie a rope properly.'

'And if she moved, your arrow could hit her,' said Catherine, who was herself an excellent archer. 'It would be far too dangerous.'

This silenced everyone. They were all aware of just how dangerous Mary's position was. Clearly they had to do something, and quickly, but it had to be a plan which they really believed would work.

'If we had something big and strong enough for her to land on, she could jump down,' said Friar Tuck. He was the chubby boy whom everyone loved and who filled the role of priest in the camp.

'What about blankets?' suggested Robin. 'If we sewed them all together and held them under the tree, would that work?'

But Marian was shaking her head. 'There isn't time,' she said. 'It would take several hours, and even then we couldn't be sure it would be strong enough.'

While they were speaking Little John was pacing around the clearing, looking carefully around, a frown on his face. To everyone's surprise, he placed a stick as tall as himself into the ground and then paced out the shadow it had made.

'Little John,' called Robin, 'what on earth are you doing? We are trying to think how we can save poor Mary.'

'That's exactly what I am doing,' answered Little John. 'Do you see that yew tree on the other side of the clearing?' He pointed to a short old tree. 'Do you see how its two thick branches form a V shape quite close to the ground? Well, wouldn't the V shape comfortably fit the top of the elm tree?'

'You mean if we chopped the elm tree down?' asked Robin.

Catherine was shaking her head. 'That's far too dangerous. It wouldn't work.'

'Yes it could,' said Michael. 'So long as the tree falls in the right direction. So long as the tree is tall enough, and I think that's what Little John is measuring now.'

Little John nodded. 'You see how this stick casts a shadow?' he said. 'The stick is three paces long and the sun casts a shadow two paces long at this moment. By measuring how many paces the elm tree's shadow is, I can work out how tall it is. Its height will be the same proportion to its shadow as the stick is to *its* shadow.'

'Ingenious!' exclaimed Friar Tuck, excitedly. Friar Tuck's mathematics were better than any of the others' and he understood exactly what Little John was saying. Even those who didn't understand the calculation realised the importance of what Little John was doing. If the elm tree was tall enough it may be possible to work out a softer landing for little Mary.

Everyone watched silently as Little John paced along the length of the elm tree's shadow, his long legs striding out as he counted.

'The shadow is fourteen paces long,' he said at last. 'Now by my calculation, the elm tree must be at least twenty-one paces tall. If the yew tree is less than that distance away from the elm, then my plan should work.'

They all counted silently as Little John carefully paced out the distance between the two trees.

'Eighteen paces,' he said, turning to them with a smile. 'I believe it will work.'

'I'm still not so sure,' said Catherine and

Marian nodded in agreement. 'What if his calculations are wrong?'

At that moment, little Mary cried out and they all looked up. One hand slipped off the branch and a gasp went out from the group on the ground. Then she managed to grab hold again.

'We *have* to do it,' said Robin, decisively. 'It's her only chance. She can't hold on much longer. Little John, get the axe.'

Little John ran to get the axe and began to swing it against the trunk of the elm, guided by Friar Tuck and Michael, the latter of whom was well-experienced in forestry crafts. The elm must be chopped at an exact angle to ensure it falls in the direction of the yew tree.

Fortunately, little Mary was on the side of the tree which would be facing upwards as the tree fell. She clung to the branch, crying, as Anna called up and explained what was going to happen.

At last Little John made the final cut and the tree swayed and tottered. Robin and Michael pushed, and to the terrified watchers it seemed to fall in slow motion, beginning with a huge cracking noise. Would the tree really fall in the direction of the yew? And could Mary hang on as it fell?

To Robin it seemed like a lifetime. He watched as Mary clung on and the tree crashed towards the ground. To the enormous relief of the band, the top of it fell into the outstretched branches of the yew. It bounced up again and then fell back to settle gently above the ground just a little less than the height of two men.

Marian was the first to react. She ran over to the far end of the elm tree and climbed up to where Mary still clung on.

'She's all right,' she called back. 'She's had a bad fright, but she's all right.'

Everyone cheered.

'We did it,' said Robin. 'Or, I should say, you did it,' he said, looking at Little John. 'Thank God for that.'

Marian came back with Mary in her arms.

'No more tree climbing for you,' said Robin, pretending to be severe.

Mary smiled through her tears and shook her head.

'And now, how are we going to sort out this mess?' said Friar Tuck, surveying the fallen tree and all the debris around it.

'I might just have an idea,' said Michael, scanning the length of the trunk. I have a plan which might just keep some of our young friends out of mischief for a while.'

NEWS FROM Abroad

2

It was the day after Mary's rescue. Robin had been meaning to make the regular trip to pick up supplies from Edwinstowe the previous day, but the visit had been delayed in all the excitement. In the weeks since they had been living in the forest he had made two trips back and each time the other children who had gone with him had carried news of themselves and the others back to eager mothers.

In return, they had received welcome supplies of cake, bread and fruit. Lizzie, the young kitchen maid, who had a soft spot for Robin, spent much of the time between each visit preparing their food. She was a very good cook so her efforts were well appreciated.

Naturally, everyone in the camp was keen to see their homes again and wanted to make the trip back, but Robin was well aware of the dangers of being caught by the Sheriff. Clearly, with fewer people travelling the danger was less and he was determined not to take any more than was necessary to help carry the supplies. He calculated that six people should be enough to carry everything. Little John, Friar Tuck, Anna and Catherine were obvious choices. Michael said he wanted to stay because he had important work to do on the fallen tree and although everyone pressed him to tell them what he planned to do, he would only smile and say:

'It's something to make sure that none of our young friends have any chance to get bored – or get into too much trouble!'

Marian would have loved to make a visit back to her own village, but everyone agreed that her recent escape from marriage to the Sheriff, thanks to Robin and his young outlaws, meant it was far too dangerous for her to leave the camp. Catherine promised she would convey news to Marian's Uncle Seth, the blacksmith.

Finally, Robin selected young William to come along with them. He was delighted. Everyone knew that he had proved himself during the rescue of Maid Marian and now he had been chosen to go on another important mission with the older ones.

As the six got their things together, Marian went to the camp gateway to check with the three children on lookout duty.

'No one has been along the path this morning except an old woman about an hour ago,' they assured her.

Marian was pleased. 'The coast's clear, Robin,' she called.

He nodded and smiled at her. Life in the camp had been even more pleasant since she had joined them after her rescue, he thought. What a beautiful young maid she was.

The lookouts pulled the rope that opened the gate. Robin and the five others crawled down the hole and up the other side of the tree trunk which hid the camp from view.

Everyone in the group except William had made the trip to Edwinstowe before and knew the rules. There must be no talking on the way so that they would be able to hear anyone approaching. If they did hear anything, the first thing to do was to take cover. It was better to be safe than sorry, and they would rather hide from people who may be friendly than risk being caught by the Sheriff's men.

Shortly after setting off they heard someone approaching and all hid amongst the trees. But it was only an old peasant woman walking by.

The next time was shortly before reaching Edwinstowe. Robin and Little John looked at each other. This time it sounded like horses' hooves. Could it be the Sheriff and his men?

In no time they were all hidden amongst the trees, well disguised in their green tunics. Robin scanned the surrounding area to satisfy himself that they could not be seen. Then he turned his eyes to the road.

Rather than men on horseback, they soon saw that it was two farmers with their herd of sheep. The sheep moved painfully slowly and in the end Robin decided that they didn't need to waste time staying hidden. He came out from behind his tree and motioned the others to do likewise.

The men were startled when six young people suddenly appeared on the path in front of them, but Robin called out.

'Have no fear, we mean you no harm. We

are just passing through the forest and didn't want to take any chances of being set upon.'

Both men relaxed but the older one called back.

'We're glad to hear it. My son and I are taking these twelve sheep to market and in these troubled times it will be a relief to get there safely and with all our sheep still with us. There are robbers everywhere and worst of all are the men sent out by our so-called Sheriff.'

Clearly these men felt the same way as Robin and his outlaws.

'We wish you a safe journey,' said Robin and the two parties carried on in their different directions.

Soon afterwards the six travellers reached Edwinstowe. They travelled the last few paces carefully and slowly. There was no point in hiding away secretly only to walk straight into a party of the Sheriff's men in their own village!

When they were sure it was safe they made their arrival known. Robin found Lizzie in the kitchen. He crept up behind her and tapped her on the shoulder. Lizzie jumped and spun round, ready to scold whoever had startled her but when she saw it was Robin, her face relaxed into a happy laugh.

'Oh Robin, it's you! And how is the brave leader of our children, then?' she said. 'He's looking every inch a young man now.'

Robin didn't mind Lizzie's teasing and he grinned affectionately back at her. At that moment his mother arrived and flung her arms around him.

It wasn't long before all the women of the village had joined in the greetings. Even Old Alfred came out to see what all the fuss was about, and Seth, the blacksmith, laid down his hammer to ask for news of his niece, Marian.

'She is well,' said Anna. 'We are all well.' The mothers smiled happily.

Everybody celebrated the news, but it was the mothers of the six young people who were happiest of all. Soon a special meal had been laid out on a table outside.

Robin insisted that they must only stay a few hours since he wanted to be back in the camp by nightfall. For the moment, however, there was time to relax and eat, and time to talk and joke, too.

Diana, Robin's mother, was the first to bring up the more serious news.

'We're so proud of the way you and your friends are managing,' she said. 'It's just as well you moved out when you did. The Sheriff becomes more greedy every day and his men regularly visit the village and take more and more food and belongings. It is so hard to satisfy the Sheriff's new tax rules and if the children were here it would be even worse. They wouldn't hesitate to threaten us to get more out of us.'

'That's awful,' said Catherine, 'don't you argue with them and complain about them taking your things?'

'Of course we do,' replied Little John's mother, 'but the answer is always the same. Whilst King Richard is imprisoned Prince John rules the country, and the word of his friend, the Sheriff of Nottingham, is law and we must obey.'

The words cast a gloom over the party. Things really were as bad as Robin had feared. He could tell by the food they'd just eaten. Things were made to look more than they were, eked out.

Robin's mother tried to restore everyone's spirits. 'I was saving this until later,' she said. 'But since we're already talking of these matters I can tell you that yesterday a messenger brought me a letter from my husband, and from the rest of the menfolk.'

The women gasped and drew closer to her, ready to grasp and cherish any small piece of news of their husbands. They were silent, looking at Diana expectantly as she drew a single sheet of parchment from her apron pocket and began to read.

'Greetings to all our loved ones,' she began in a strong, clear voice. 'At the time I write this letter we have been travelling for over two weeks. All of us are well, although our feet are sore from walking through the fields of northern France. We are in good spirits because we believe we will rescue King Richard. Our belief is strengthened by some good fortune we ran into in Normandy, just after landing in France.'

Diana paused to look round at the listening group. Little John ran to fetch her a stool and she sat on it and took up the letter again.

'As we walked through a small village,' she read, 'we found a good knight in a great deal of trouble. Gangs of ruffians had tripped up his horse and were about to rob the knight. There were may more of us than there were ruffians and we arrived just in time to scare them off. The good knight was grateful to us and gave us food and shelter for the night. When we told him of our mission to rescue the King he insisted on giving us two hundred gold sovereigns towards it.

'Now we really believe we will be successful in our crusade and are in good heart. Of course we constantly think of our women and children and we pray God will keep you safe.

'Diana, please tell Robin that we are particularly proud of him and wish him well in keeping the children safe. We hope all the children can benefit by seeing how important it is for people to stand up for what they believe in. When there is dishonesty, fight it with the truth. When there is unfairness, fight it with justice. And when there is selfishness, fight it with charity.

'We love you all, and look forward to the day when we meet again.

'Signed Christopher Hood and the men of Edwinstowe.'

Diana's voice broke as she read the last two lines and the hand holding the letter dropped into her lap. Robin sprang forward to put an arm around his mother's shoulders.

'They will be back,' he said. 'We shall succeed.' But there was more confidence in his voice than there was in his heart.

cry wolf!

There was silence when Diana finished reading. Then Friar Tuck began to quietly clap his hands together. Quickly everyone else joined in until they all sat applauding the letter from their menfolk.

It was an emotional moment, particularly for Robin. His father had spoken directly to him in the letter. More than that though, he realised that every word was meant especially for him. In his father's absence it was up to him to lead the fight for honesty, justice and charity. He decided then and there that he and the others would do more to fight the evil Sheriff. He looked round at the faces of his friends and neighbours and felt even greater determination that the children's camp would become more than just a hide-away. It would become the headquarters of the fight against the Sheriff of Nottingham.

After all, he thought, he and his gang of children did have an advantage over everyone else in the county. They had chosen to hide themselves away so that they could live outside the Sheriff's unfair laws. They had turned themselves into outlaws who could not easily be tracked down by the Sheriff's men. Now they must use this advantage to strike back for everything that the good men of Edwinstowe were away fighting for.

Robin was certain that in Little John, Friar Tuck, Marian, Anna and Catherine he had a team capable of doing much to upset the Sheriff's plans. Hadn't they shown how they could effectively outwit him when they had rescued Maid Marian?

There was one other major issue and that was the amount of time spent looking after the younger children. If only they could find a way to keep them occupied more, and so leave the older ones to devote more time and energy in outwitting the Sheriff and his men.

'Robin, have you gone quite deaf?' His mother interrupted his thoughts. 'I've been talking to you for the last two minutes but you seem to be dreaming! Isn't it time you set off back to the camp? It will be dark in two hours or so.'

Robin nodded, hugged his mother and picked up their provisions. The others did the same, promising to convey last minute messages to the other children. They waved until their mothers were out of sight and then walked on, glad to be silent and lost in their thoughts of sadness at leaving their homes again, but also pride at the news of their fathers' adventures.

After walking for over an hour, they rounded a bend and suddenly came upon the two shepherds they had met earlier. This time the two men were sitting on the edge of the path with nine of their sheep wandering around them.

'Hello again,' called Robin. 'How is your journey going?'

'Not well,' said the older man. 'If you had been here ten minutes ago you would have seen us dealing with some of the Sheriff's men. Their leader told us that a new law has been made which states that we must pay a tax for walking our sheep on this path. We tried to argue but there was nothing we could do. In the end they took three of our twelve sheep. How are we to make a living when the Sheriff can make up a rule to rob us just like that?'

'But this is terrible!' said Anna, laying down her bundle and looking at Robin. 'What was it your father said?'

Robin was nodding his head. 'I say it's up to outlaws like ourselves to stop this, but how are we going to do it?'

'What we need to do,' said Little John, 'is to drive the sheep away from the soldiers and then catch them when they run off. A couple of us need to get ahead of the soldiers and then find a way to scare the sheep so that they run on ahead.'

'It's a good plan, Little John,' said Robin, 'but how can we scare the sheep enough to make them run off?'

It was William who provided the answer. Without warning he let his head drop back and let out an ear-splitting howl. It sounded just like the cry of a hungry wolf. Nothing was guaranteed to make sheep run faster than that sound.

'Young William is proving his value yet again,' smiled Robin. 'Now, who is to go ahead?'

30

'I don't believe they would give any trouble to a young monk,' said Friar Tuck. 'Let us catch up with them together and then I alone will hurry past. I'll wait a short way ahead and collect the sheep when they run off, and then put them on a rope and hide in the bushes until the soldiers give up their search.'

It was a clever plan and everyone hoped it would work. For the next ten minutes they ran quietly along the path. It was fortunate that the soldiers had stopped for a rest a little further on because Friar Tuck was almost exhausted by the time they spotted them on the path.

Everyone else held back whilst he hurried past. Sure enough the soldiers did not stop the young monk passing by. As soon as he was ahead and out of sight. William began to make his wolf sounds.

Robin and the others watched from behind the trees. They saw the sheep prick up their ears and then pause for a moment before charging off along the path. The soldiers got up and gave chase until one tripped over a tree root and the others stopped to help him.

31

The sheep disappeared round the bend. Robin grinned across at Little John. The plan was working!

'We'll wait,' whispered Robin. 'We can't risk the soldiers coming back.'

So they sat, out of sight of the path, for over an hour before continuing on. There was no sign of the soldiers or Friar Tuck and the three sheep.

'I hear something!' said William at last and they all listened intently. Sure enough, there was a bleating sound from somewhere up ahead and a few seconds later a smiling Friar Tuck appeared pulling a rope to which the three sheep were attached.

'We are greatly in your debt,' said the older shepherd, turning to Robin. 'I can't thank you and your outlaws enough. Today you have scored a victory against the Sheriff and set an example to us all.'

It was dark when they finally reached the camp and everyone was waiting anxiously and clamoured to hear of their adventures.

'Tomorrow,' said Robin. 'We are all too tired to do it justice. I'm sure you have much to tell us also.'

Michael grinned across at Marian. His

surprise would have to wait until morning too.

Adventures All Round

4

It was several hours after dawn when Robin finally woke up. He had not slept so well for weeks. He opened his eyes so see Marian bending over him with a bowl of fruit and nuts. Everything seemed perfect.

He smiled up at her and then sat up, taking the broad leaf which served as a plate.

'The children gathered these yesterday,' she said, 'and kept the choicest for you, our leader.'

There was also a large slice of bread, freshly baked by Michael in the fire oven he had made.

'Sit beside me while I eat,' said Robin.

So she sat, and between mouthfuls he told her of their visit to Edwinstowe and his father's letter. Then he recounted their adventures with the sheep.

'So you fooled the Sheriff yet again,' she laughed, and Robin felt a tremendous happiness as he looked into her radiant face. For a moment, there was silence between them as they looked at each other. Then the spell was broken and he looked away.

'Something is troubling you,' she said, resting a hand on his arm.

'Two things,' he said. 'The sheep for a start. But we must find more ways to fight the Sheriff. It's our duty to do all we can. I promised my father that we should stand up for justice, honesty and charity while he was away and we need a plan to do this. We can't just hope to stumble across opportunities.'

'You're not doing too badly,' laughed Marian, leaving her hand on his arm. 'It isn't just the sheep you saved. If it hadn't been for you and your outlaws, I would have been the unhappiest wife in the world.'

And I the unhappiest man, thought Robin, but did not speak the words aloud.

'You said there were two things,' she went on. 'What else is bothering you?'

Robin took a deep breath and sighed. 'We have two jobs to do. We must find ways to fight the Sheriff but at the same time we must look after the younger children and keep them safe. To do this we must keep them busy and not let them get bored. Look what happened to Mary. Now that the camp is more or less finished there's only the look-out duty and the corn to tend. No more ditches to dig or walls to build.'

As he was speaking Marian's smile broadened into a grin.

'I don't see what's funny,' he said. 'It seems we have to spend most of our time amusing the children and meanwhile the Sheriff will get away with everything.'

Marian was still laughing and shaking her head. 'Oh Robin, that's one worry less for you. We have something to show you. In fact, the whole camp has been waiting for you to wake up.'

She took his hand and pulled him to his feet. Then, still hand in hand, she took him towards the centre of the clearing.

At first all Robin could see was the huge tree which lay across the clearing from one side to the other. At the far end of it stood Michael, Little John, Anna, Catherine and all the children of the camp.

As they saw Robin approaching the younger children started to cheer.

'What's happening?' Robin asked, looking at Little John.

'I think you'd better speak to Michael,' said Little John. 'It is he who came up with the idea which will keep our little friends busy.'

Again, there were cheers and Michael blushed as he came forward.

'The idea came to me yesterday,' he said. 'I was trying to work out how to cut the tree up into smaller pieces and then I noticed that some of the branches were a perfect shape for sliding down. All that was needed was to cut and shape them so that they were flat on the top side of the branch. Then the wood could be worked smooth and we would have slides for the children to play on. Everyone helped, so it didn't take long.'

He pointed to the tree and Robin saw that it didn't look at all like the tree that had been lying there the previous morning.

'Once the slides were made,' continued Michael, 'I began to wonder what else we could do with the tree and the results are there. It seems to be very popular with the children, anyway,' he finished, shyly.

Robin looked at the tree with amazement while everyone stood silently watching his reaction.

Huge smooth play slides hung down from

each side and there were many other inventions too. From the underside of two other big branches Michael had hung loops of rope. With pieces of wood attached to each of them they became six perfectly good swings. Hanging down from the main trunk was a web of knotted rope forming a huge rope ladder.

Robin looked more closely at the top of the tree.

'You've added more branches and bound them together,' he said. 'It's the best climbing frame I've ever seen.'

'And watch this,' said Marian. She waved to little Mary who climbed up the roots which stuck high in the air. Michael had attached a rope and pulley system. Mary sat in the loop provided and glided safely down to the lower end of the rope which was attached to the base of a tree at the other side of the clearing.

Robin said nothing for several minutes and Michael said, nervously, 'It was just an idea I had. So that the children could have their own little adventures.'

Robin laughed and clapped his hands. 'It's amazing, Michael! I can't believe what you've done in just one day. It's a perfect adventure playground, exciting but not dangerous. One day all children will want one of these!'

It was the signal that the children had been waiting for. Cheering loudly, they raced up the fallen tree trunk. Seconds later they were all over it like a swarm of insects, running and jumping, sliding and climbing while Robin and his outlaws looked on happily.

'Now the children are having their little adventures,' said Little John, summing up their feelings. 'All we have to work out is how we are going to plan our bigger ones. The only difference is, our adventures will be real!'

They didn't have long to wait. As they sat on the grass watching the children play, their pleasure was interrupted by three owl hoots.

Robin and Little John got to their feet quickly. It was the call from the lookouts which meant 'Beware! Possible danger!' They ran to the front gate of the camp, followed more slowly by the others. Even the children had noticed something was wrong and had jumped down from the tree and stood watching expectantly.

William crouched behind the tree trunk

which was the main lookout tower, his finger to his lips.

Robin sprang up beside him and William pointed, wordlessly.

There, not twenty paces away, was a group of soldiers on horseback. As Robin and William watched, holding their breath, one of the soldiers dismounted and pulled out a roll of parchment. From his pocket he pulled a nail and then used the handle of his sword to nail the parchment to the tree trunk. Then he mounted his horse and the soldiers all rode off again.

Robin stared at the notice on the tree. Even from where he crouched he could plainly see the colourful crest of the Sheriff of Nottingham. He scrambled down to join the others.

'The Sheriff's men are nailing notices to trees. This may be just the adventure we're looking for! William, please go and fetch the notice.'

joining the tax tour

5

Everybody gathered close as Robin spread the notice out on an old tree stump. Even those who could not read stared at the large black letters. Written notices were rare, so it must be very important.

'Citizens of Nottinghamshire must be aware of the new Tax Laws,' read Robin in a voice loud enough for all to hear. 'All citizens are required to pay directly to me all coins, jewellery and precious metals which they own. A special taxation tour is already taking place. My soldiers' Treasure Train will visit all villages in the county and payment must be immediate. Any attempt to hide money will result in severe punishment. The villages will be taxed as listed below. Signed, the Sheriff of Nottingham.'

Robin looked up, his face stricken. 'It lists the villages below with the dates of the visits.'

'Visits!' shouted Little John. 'I don't call that visits! I call it highway robbery!' He looked over Robin's shoulder. 'Look where they will visit tomorrow. Our village of Edwinstowe. They must be stopped. Robin, we must think of a plan!'

'Yes, we must warn them,' said Catherine.

'There's no point in that,' said Robin. 'They cannot risk hiding anything from the Sheriff's men. But I do have a plan which means that it doesn't matter how much they take from Edwinstowe or any other village.'

Catherine gasped and opened her mouth to speak but Robin held up his hand.

'Wait until you hear of my plan. We are going to join the Treasure Train with the sergeant's permission! Then we will find a way of giving back all that they have stolen.'

They all stared at Robin. It was a daring and very dangerous idea. Little John was the first to react.

'Count me in, Robin. I'm not afraid to take the risk. I will do anything to foil the evil Sheriff's plans.'

'Thank you, Little John,' said Robin, patting him on the back. 'I knew I would have your support.'

'And mine,' said Michael quickly. 'I shall be glad to come.'

'You too,' said Robin. 'For my plan to work, it needs your special way with animals.'

Michael was delighted. What a great adventure, and he would be in the thick of it!

'How and when are we going to join the Treasure Train?' asked Little John, leaning against the fallen trunk. 'This will certainly need careful planning.'

'And how can we steal the treasure back?' asked Michael. 'That will be the most difficult part.'

'And that is the question I don't yet know the answer to,' replied Robin. 'But I believe it will become clear to us when we are properly part of the train. As for your question, Little John, we shall join the Treasure Train tomorrow morning. It is due to visit Edwinstowe and will pass along our path on the way. With a little help from the younger children, we shall join the tour then.'

Little John was shaking his head. 'It would seem foolhardy to start this plan without having any clear idea of how to carry it through.'

'Trust me, Little John,' said Robin. 'In the

meantime, let me explain what will happen tomorrow.'

He gave a detailed explanation of his plan for joining the Treasure Train and listened to improvements suggested by the others. Eventually they had a plan which they all believed would work and even Little John seemed more confident about the outcome.

Robin had a sleepless night and was relieved to see dawn break the following morning. As he put on his green outfit he felt in the pocket and drew out a small leather purse. Old Alfred had given it to him and it contained a lucky four-leafed clover. Anna had taken it with her when she had helped to rescue Maid Marian. Now Robin hoped it would bring him luck, too. He fingered the soft leather thoughtfully and then put it back into his pocket and went to have some breakfast.

When they were ready the three adventurers said their goodbyes. Everyone wished them luck and Marian reached shyly up and kissed Robin on the cheek.

'God be with you,' she whispered.

The three of them left the camp and took up their positions a little way along the path.

Shorty afterwards, William and two other young boys took up their own places further back.

Everybody waited nervously for the sound of horses' hooves.

'There will probably be at least twenty men, I should think,' said Robin.

Little John nodded. 'It would be the Sheriff's style to intimidate people with numbers, but at least we shall hear them coming well enough.'

It was almost an hour before they heard anything. Then Robin signalled to William and he signalled back that they were ready.

The noise of hooves became louder and louder. Robin's heart thumped. This was it; there was no turning back.

As the first line of soldiers came into sight, William and his two friends sprang into action. They ran across the path shouting and yelling and acting as if they were just a gang of boys chasing and generally playing noisily.

It took the soldiers and their horses completely by surprise. The nearest horse panicked and threw its rider to the ground. Then it galloped off along the path whilst the boys disappeared back into the bushes.

The soldiers cursed and one or two shook their fists in the direction of the boys. The soldier who had been thrown off was already back on his feet and looking round for his horse. Instead he saw Robin and Little John, in their green outfits, further up the path.

Michael had gone to find the horse. One of his many skills was in comforting horses. All he had to do was whistle softly and the horse became aware of him. It turned and looked back at him curiously. Michael whistled again. This time it began walking slowly towards him and when it was close enough, he grabbed hold of the reins.

The unmounted soldier and his company had watched silently as Michael brought the horse forward, talking softly to it.

'You have a way with horses,' said the sergeant. 'Thank you for your help. If you hadn't been here we would have lost that horse, thanks to those wretched children. I've a good mind to lock them up for a couple of days. That might knock some of that spirit out of them.' He grinned at the others. 'Maybe their parents would pay richly to get them back.'

There was a rumble of laughter amongst

the rest of the company and Robin spoke quickly. 'Sir, you have seen my friend's skill with horses, and my other friend and I are cooks.' He indicated to Little John standing beside him. 'The estate where we worked was burnt down and we are looking for work. Do you know of anyone who may need the services of a groom and two willing cooks?' The carefully rehearsed words rolled off his tongue and he hoped they sounded genuine.

For a moment nobody spoke and Robin began to fear the worst.

'Well, he's the largest cook I've ever seen!' said the sergeant, looking at Little John. 'It speaks well for his cooking!' Again his men laughed. 'You could join us for a few days. We are touring the county gathering taxes for the Sheriff. It is hard and hungry work and we could do with better food than Henry here serves up.'

The men cheered and turned to someone in their midst.

'It's not my fault,' said the man. 'I never said I was a cook. I would be happier than anyone if these two young lads would take over the chore.'

Robin, Little John and Michael grinned. 'Then we gladly accept, Sir,' said Robin.

He could hardly believe it. The first part of their plan was a success and they were a part of the Treasure Train.

Now all they had to do was find a way to steal the treasure back!

tax collection

6

Since the three outlaws had no horses of their own, they were told to sit in the open cart. Eight soldiers rode in front and eight behind, then two on either side making a total of twenty men plus an old man driving the cart.

As Robin climbed on to the cart he could see that most of the space was taken up with a huge padlocked iron chest. Michael managed to squeeze down beside the driver but Robin and Little John had no option but to sit right on top of the chest.

They set off again through the forest. William and his friends had obviously got safely back inside the camp, so that was one less worry. Robin watched the soldiers chatting as they rode along. They probably saw this as a chance to spend a few pleasant days in the countryside. They were under the Sheriff's orders and even if they questioned the justice in what they were doing, they had no option but to obey.

They soon arrived in a small village called Greenmere, which was about halfway between their camp and Edwinstowe. It was a pretty village made up of about seven or eight cottages on the edge of a small lake. Luckily, Robin was not known here so there was no chance of recognition. Nevertheless, all three turned their faces away as they pulled into the centre where the villagers were already waiting for the soldiers.

A man of about fifty stepped forward and spoke politely but coldly to the sergeant.

'We have the Sheriff's money ready,' he said. 'We can ill afford it but you will see that everything is here. This is what you asked for.' He pointed to a pile of gold coins and a few bits of jewellery. 'Please take it and leave us to our work.'

'Good,' replied the sergeant. 'But while this is put into the treasure chest I'm sure you will not mind if my men have a look round. You would be surprised how many times people seem to forget things. We often find them in the most unlikely places!'

Four soldiers were ordered to load the

treasure into the chest and four more were dispatched to search the village. Robin and Little John obligingly moved off the chest and climbed down into the road, keeping well concealed behind the cart. The padlock was unlocked and the lid of the chest raised.

They watched, horrified, as the soldiers pushed past people to get to the houses. One man protested and was knocked to the ground. A woman who would not move from her doorway was picked up and lifted out of the way.

Robin and Little John looked at each other, both feeling so helpless and even more determined to succeed in their plan.

Suddenly there was a shout of triumph and one of the soldiers walked out of the cottage at the end of the row waving a gold necklace.

'Look what I found!' he shouted. 'It was kept in such a strange place too, halfway up the chimney!'

'Whose cottage is that?' bellowed the sergeant.

No one answered. Then, slowly, an old woman shuffled forward. She was almost bent double as she clutched her back and was so tiny that her head barely reached up to the belly of the sergeant's horse.

'It's mine,' she said, quietly yet firmly. 'I'm an old woman. My grandmother passed this necklace on to me on my wedding day and I promised that I would pass it to my own granddaughter on her wedding day.'

At that moment, a girl of about fifteen rushed forward and flung her arms round the old woman.

'Oh Nana!' she cried. 'You shouldn't have hidden the necklace for me.' She turned to the sergeant. 'Please don't punish her,' she pleaded. 'She's an old woman and doesn't know what she's doing.'

'She knows well enough,' said the sergeant. 'Everyone must obey the Sheriff's orders. His needs are greater than yours. Those who disobey must be punished as an example to others.'

He clicked his fingers and two soldiers dismounted and ran towards the old woman's house. At the doorway they grabbed a handful of hay. Then, pulling a flint out of his pocket, one of them lit the hay and it flared brightly.

'Oh no, please don't!' wailed the old woman. The girl said nothing but held her grandmother close and wept silently.

The sergeant laughed and signalled the

soldier to go ahead. Seconds later the cottage was on fire, the flames roaring joyously at the thatched roof. The villagers could only stand by silently and watch as, in a few minutes, the home where the woman had lived all her life was destroyed.

As the last wall fell the soldiers cheered and remounted their horses, ready to ride on. Robin and Little John climbed back on to the cart, feeling totally sick. Robin noticed that the sergeant had turned to look at them as if judging their reaction. He nudged Little John and Michael and they all stretched their mouths into forced laughter. Anything else would have made the sergeant suspicious but it was the hardest bit of acting any of them had ever had to do.

Satisfied, the sergeant gave the signal to move on. 'We have no more time to waste on this village,' he said. 'We must be in Edwinstowe well before nightfall.'

As they set off again Robin and Little John spoke in low voices.

'We shall have to act quickly when we reach Edwinstowe,' said Robin. 'We cannot depend on everyone not to give us away. It will be such a shock to see us.'

'We must warn them about not hiding anything, too,' whispered Little John. 'I couldn't bear it if anyone's house was burnt down there.'

'One of us must find a way to go ahead and prepare them,' said Robin. 'And I think I have a plan.'

When they were within ten minutes of the village they put the plan into action. Robin slumped to the floor of the cart, clutching his stomach and groaning loudly.

Little John called out to the sergeant.

'My friend is ill. He complains of stomach ache and thinks it may be something he ate.'

'What a shame,' the sergeant shouted back, unsympathetically. 'We can't stop. He will have to wait until we reach the village.'

Robin and Little John exchanged glances. This was exactly the answer they had hoped for. Robin continued to play along, lying on the floor of the cart. Then, as they came within sight of the village he groaned more loudly and leaned over the side of the cart.

'I can't wait. I must go now!' He leapt off the moving cart and began running as fast as he could, ahead of the Treasure Train and into the village. The soldiers laughed, slowing the party down a little and giving Robin valuable extra seconds.

'One of you should go with him,' said the sergeant. 'We don't know this fellow.'

'But Sir,' laughed his second in command, 'he is in too much of a hurry to linger talking to anyone.'

Robin ran straight into the kitchen and bumped into an amazed Lizzie, who started to speak before Robin gestured her to silence.

'Little John, Michael and I are here with the Sheriff's men. No one must give any sign that they recognise us and no one must hide anything. The soldiers will search everywhere. If they find anything they will destroy the whole village.'

Lizzie's face went white. 'The golden goblet is in the chimney in the dining room. Your mother wouldn't hear of it being given to the Sheriff.'

'Oh no,' sighed Robin. 'The chimney is the first place they will look...'

Robin broke off in mid sentence as horses' hooves could be heard in the courtyard. With a last look at Lizzie, he walked back outside, still clutching his stomach.

The sergeant glanced at him and seemed satisfied when Robin climbed back on the cart.

'Feeling better, I hope?' he asked. 'We shall need your services tonight as we'll be hungry after all this excitement. And we trust you will not poison us?' He let out a roar of laughter before turning his attention to his task.

'People of Edwinstowe!' he shouted. 'Come out where we can see you and bring the Sheriff's treasure with you. Woe betide anyone who tries to hide anything from us.'

Robin looked at Little John and Michael and hoped that Lizzie had managed to warn enough of the others for the news to spread. They would soon find out, as the villagers were already beginning to walk out into the courtyard.

naughty william saves the day

7

For several moments nothing happened. Then Robin's mother appeared in the main doorway. The other women followed her in an orderly fashion. Last of all came Seth and Old Alfred. The latter walked even more slowly than usual, helped by two of the older women.

Robin caught his mother's eye. She looked straight at him without giving any sign of recognition. He breathed a sigh of relief as the other women did likewise. Clearly Lizzie had managed to warn them in time. But Robin had not reckoned on the smallest children. Only the children over four years old had gone to the camp and that left several younger ones. Now a small girl called Ruth waved her hand at him.

'Bobbin!' she shouted. 'Bobbin!'

The sergeant turned to look at the three

young men. 'This child seems to know one of you. I did not ask where you were from. An omission it seems.'

Little John tried to grin nonchalantly. In a minute the sergeant would put two and two together and see through Robin's little act.

But the child's mother was laughing and shaking her head. 'Oh no, Sir. These lads are strangers to us. One of them looks a little like my nephew, Robert, and Ruth is very fond of him, that's all.'

It was a weak explanation and Robin prayed that the sergeant would forget the episode.

It was Diana who came to the rescue.

'We owe nothing!' she said. 'But we realise we have no choice but to pay everything you ask. I wonder how you can live with yourself after carrying out these unfair laws.'

The sergeant turned to her, red with anger. 'Just bring forth your treasures, Madam, and less of the impertinence, else we carry out more than you have bargained for!'

Diana Hood stood her ground, listening to his ranting with a defiant air.

Once again Robin and Little John climbed down from the treasure chest while it was opened and filled. He watched in dismay as money and valuables from his own village were thrown in.

But the women were deliberately slow and he soon realised what was going on. There was no sign of Lizzie yet, but Robin was sure that at this very minute she was running to the dining room to fetch the golden goblet from its hiding place.

Sure enough, Lizzie appeared at the doorway and then sidled up to the table on which were piled a heap of gold coins. Then, watching the sergeant all the time, she carefully threw what looked like a bundle of rags on to the table. Robin was in no doubt that it was the goblet wrapped in cloth. He caught Lizzie's eye and she gave a tiny nod.

After the awful house-burning in Greenmere, Robin was relieved that everything went as well as possible in Edwinstowe. Watching the soldiers' faces, he could see what delight they took in robbing the women and wondered what sort of men they could be to revel in such a task. They searched every corner and every chimney but found nothing, to the obvious disappointment of the sergeant, who no doubt would have found an excuse to punish the villagers had it not been for the lateness of the hour. Robin also suspected, deep down, that his mother would have enjoyed further arguments with the man but the consequences were too great.

The Treasure Train set off again. Robin, Little John and Michael left their village poor but unharmed.

'Well done,' Michael whispered to Robin. 'I hated seeing the soldiers robbing our village but there was nothing we could do – yet.'

They were all silent as they rattled on in the cart. How to get the treasure back. That was the real problem, the one they didn't yet have a plan for. They didn't have much time either, judging by the fullness of the chest. Soon the Treasure Train would have to return to Nottingham to deposit the treasure before starting out again, and Robin could not risk being recognised by the Sheriff.

He was staring idly at the bushes to the left of the track when he thought he was imagining things. It looked like William's face, peering out at them. He blinked and looked again and then nudged Little John and Michael. It *was* William! He was running through the bushes, keeping up with the Treasure Train and watching it all the way.

What was he doing here, Robin thought, furiously. They had not asked him to do this. Not only was he putting himself in danger, but also if he were caught it could make the sergeant suspicious of he and his two friends.

'Wait until we get back to camp!' muttered Robin under his breath. 'I'm going to deal with that little fool! He deserves horse-whipping!'

The sergeant called a halt. They were in a small clearing at the base of a hill. There was an area of flat dry land surrounded on all sides by thick trees and bushes. Above them there was cover from the massive branches of a huge old oak tree.

'This is our camp for the night!' shouted the sergeant. He turned to Michael. 'Take the horses for food and water. Two of my men will unload the cart.'

All the men dismounted and Robin, Little John and Michael jumped down from the cart. Michael began unhitching the horses while four soldiers came and motioned to the other two to help with unloading the chest. It was incredibly heavy and they could only drag it slowly towards the edge of the cart and then dump it on the ground where it fell.

71

Before Robin and Little John could do anything about William, they found the sergeant standing in front of them.

'Now you two can start earning your keep,' he said. 'I hope for your sake that you can cook as well as you said you could. We have had a hard day and need something better than the rubbish we had last night.'

Robin was suddenly alarmed. He had never cooked anything in his life. He looked at Little John.

'Just do as I say,' Little John whispered, and began unloading the barrels of food. 'I know more than enough to keep these men happy.'

Within two hours the soldiers were tucking into a delicious stew.

'It was lucky that we found you,' shouted one of them. The others joined in, praising Robin and Little John's cooking. Robin smiled and began collecting up the wooden plates.

At last their chores were over and everyone was settling down for the night. Exhausted, the three sat down to talk. Something had to be done tonight. They couldn't go through another day of helping to rob villages.

'But how on earth are we going to steal something which takes six men to lift?' asked

Robin. 'Even with you, Little John, doing the work of two men, it would be impossible, and the noise would be awful. The soldiers would catch us long before we got very far.'

'What if we made a ramp and slid the chest up on to the cart in the middle of the night?' suggested Michael. 'We could harness up the horses and then drive off.'

'Too noisy and still too slow,' said Little John. 'Stealing that iron chest is going to require a very clever trick indeed.'

Robin got to his feet. 'But in the meantime, I'm going to get hold of that fool William and tell him what I think of him.' He walked off towards the edge of the clearing. He would enjoy letting his temper loose on the boy. He could have led them all into disaster.

'Wait!' Little John had sprung up and run after him, grabbing him by the arm. 'William is our contact with the others. If we can get their help, I have an idea which just might work. It's not going to be easy but by choosing this particular camp site, the sergeant might just have given us a chance.'

Robin looked puzzled but followed him back to where they had been sitting.

'Do you see that huge branch right above

us,' said Little John, pointing. 'It's at least as thick as a man's waist.'

Robin and Michael nodded.

'I think it would hold the weight of our treasure chest, don't you?'

'Why yes,' answered Robin, 'but I don't see...'

Little John began to explain his plan. The key now was to make contact with William and tell him about it without being seen by the soldiers.

Most of the soldiers were lying relaxing on their blankets, talking quietly or sleeping. Nobody paid any attention to Robin as he walked towards the edge of the clearing again. Nor did they notice that it was he who then made three low owl hoots.

Instantly there was a similar reply. William had picked up the signal and answered with his own.

Robin held a scrap of parchment on which he had written a note. He stooped and picked up a large stone. Then, after wrapping the note around the stone, he casually swung back his arm and lobbed it into the bushes at the point where he judged William's owl hoots had come from.

A few seconds later, a single hoot came back to Robin. William had got the message. Now all they had to do was wait and hope that William would succeed in carrying out the instructions. If all went well, he would fetch the outlaws to arrive by two hours after midnight. Then they would see whether Little John's clever plan would work.

Little John's Magic Trick

8

The hours passed slowly. Everyone was tired after their long day and soon all the soldiers stopped talking and there was silence except for the snoring and the occasional rustle of leaves as a soldier turned in his sleep.

'Why don't you sleep for a while,' Michael said to Robin and Little John. 'I'll have my turn later.'

Michael felt strangely calm as he sat in the dark forest. He knew they were about to take a huge risk, but somehow nothing seemed real sitting there awake and alone. There was no point in worrying about what they were going to do. It was their duty, and he admired Robin enormously for the strength of his convictions.

He struggled against sleep, unwilling to wake the others, and had almost decided to waken one of them when he heard the sound he had been waiting for. Three soft hoots rang out from the edge of the clearing.

Michael answered with a single owl hoot and then shook Robin and Little John awake. The three of them quietly rose and crept towards the edge of the clearing, straining their eyes to see where William and the others were. Luck was still with them and at that moment the clouds parted, bathing the forest in the light of a full moon.

Standing at the edge of the forest were the outlaws. There was Friar Tuck – they could tell him by his shape – and William, Anna, Catherine, Marian and three or four other young helpers.

Robin motioned for them to stay where they were, except for the young lad who had brought his bow and arrows. Then he crept to the cart and took out a very long, thick coil of rope which had been lying in the cart throughout their journey and had provided the inspiration for Little John's plan. He carefully tied one end of the rope round the handle on top of the chest. The other end of the rope he tightly fixed to an arrow.

Now came the moment of truth. Taking up

his bow, he fitted the arrow into the bowstring and took aim, pointing it almost straight up into the sky. Then he released the arrow.

The bowstring made a soft hum as it sprang back and it seemed it must wake one of the soldiers only a few paces away, but nobody stirred and Robin's eyes were on his arrow, soaring high into the air. As it descended, it looped over the huge branch above them.

They all watched with bated breath as the arrow continued to descend towards the group at the edge of the forest, trailing its tail of rope, and coming to rest just above their heads. Then they saw the figure of Catherine reach up and grab the arrow and several others got hold of the rope and pulled it tight.

Robin, Michael and Little John grinned at each other other in delight. The first part of the plan was complete. The treasure chest was fastened to the rope, which hung over the huge branch. Now if they all had enough strength, they could pull the chest up until it was suspended high up in the tree. There it would remain until they came back for it. And who would think of looking up in a tree? The soldiers would never be able to work out how the chest had been stolen, it would seem as if it had disappeared by magic. And, although it would look suspicious that the three of them should disappear at the same time, there was no alternative. Their time with the Treasure Train was thankfully at an end.

That was the plan, but it all depended on whether they had the strength to pull the chest up.

'I shall go and help them,' said Little John.

'I'm sure it will work,' Michael said. 'My father and I have many times lifted heavy bags of flour this way.'

Robin knew that in theory, using a pulley system, such as the branch and rope, allowed people to lift weights heavier than they normally could, but there was always a limit and that chest was very heavy.

Little John crept round to help. His great strength would make a big difference. At first it didn't seem as if it would work. They strained and pulled and only managed to pull the chest a little way off the ground. Robin and Michael hardly dared breathe as twigs around the chest made small popping noises as the chest's weight shifted from them.

The first bit was the most difficult. Once the chest was off the ground, it would become much easier to pull up.

'I'll go and help too,' said Michael. He began to edge his way from the centre of the clearing. Suddenly it happened. There was an almighty CRACK as he trod on a stick. He immediately turned and ran back and flung himself down on his blanket next to Robin.

Through half-closed eyes, Robin watched the sleeping forms of the soldiers, praying that none of them would waken. But their luck had run out. The sergeant was stumbling to his feet and looking round, trying to work out where the noise had come from. He seemed just about to give up and lie down again when he saw it. The empty patch where the treasure chest should have been. Rubbing his eyes in disbelief, he stared at the spot. Then he jumped to his feet and shouted.

'Wake up! Wake up everyone! We've been robbed, you lazy idiots. We've been robbed.'

Within seconds every soldier was on his feet. Robin and Michael stood there too, trying to blend in and aware of the missing Little John. The soldiers also stared at the place where the chest had been. All that could be seen in the moonlight, however, was the depression in the ground which its weight had made. It was as if it had been removed by magic.

Robin and Michael stood, hearts thumping, sweating with fear even in the chill of the night. They were caught! Their plan had failed. At any moment the chest would come crashing down and they would all be discovered.

Robin had been entrusted with the safety of the children but instead he had got them into far more danger.

prisoners

9

The chest did not come down. The outlaws had managed to secure it and escape after all. The problem now was, how were Robin and Michael going to escape, especially when the sergeant discovered that Little John was no longer with them.

Without waiting for daylight, the sergeant organised them into four separate search parties. Each group had to search a neighbouring area of the forest for signs of the theft. Ironically, Robin and Michael's group was ordered to search the very spot above which the chest was suspended. Neither of them dared look up to check.

All the soldiers were clear about one thing. There would be trouble if the chest was not found. Henry, the ex-cook, was in charge of Robin and Michael's party and was the first to notice that Little John was not with them.

'Oh, he was allocated to one of the other search parties,' said Robin, which seemed to satisfy Henry.

The boys were impressed at the thoroughness of the search. It seemed that every blade of grass and every twig was examined for clues, and as time went on, the boys became more and more nervous that the way Henry was carrying out his search, it seemed quite likely that he would look up into the tree and see the chest hanging there.

Robin toyed with the idea of distracting Henry somehow, yet that would draw attention to themselves, which he didn't want to do.

He was saved the decision by a yell from the camp.

'Breakfast! Sergeant's orders!'

The soldiers didn't need telling twice. Night had turned into day and they'd been searching for several hours.

Nevertheless, breakfast only consisted of bread and ale, which fortunately didn't require the cooks' assistance.

'I think it's better if we remain separate,' said Robin to Michael. 'That way Little John's absence won't be so easily noticed.'

While his men were eating, the sergeant stood up.

'It seems clear to me that somehow thieves have already escaped with our treasure chest and that it's a waste of time searching this area any more. We shall find both the chest and the thieves, have no fear, and when we do, they'll wish they had never been born. What's more, if I find that anyone within this camp has had anything to do with it...'

It wasn't necessary for him to say what he would do. Robin went cold with fear. It would obviously be something very nasty indeed. Traitors were never dealt with lightly.

'We will search for as long as it takes,' went on the sergeant, 'and we'll use as many men as we need. I sent a messenger to the Sheriff early this morning and I believe that he himself will lead a company of men who should be here shortly. I know every one of you will co-operate with our Sheriff.'

Robin and Michael couldn't believe their ears. The Sheriff would certainly recognise Robin. They had to get away quickly.

But it was too late. The sound of horses' hooves clattered along the path. Robin saw Michael's stricken face and tried to give him a look of encouragement. There was nothing more he could do now, no plan to get them out of trouble. He was helpless.

Twelve soldiers on horseback trotted into the clearing and at their centre was the Sheriff. He was just as Robin remembered him – a cruel-looking man with a dark beard and staring eyes.

Now he was staring at Robin. There was a puzzled expression on his face as if he was trying to place where he'd seen him before.

As the sergeant welcomed the Sheriff and his men, the Sheriff paid little attention. He still stared at Robin.

'I recognise that boy,' he yelled to the sergeant. 'Who is he? How does he come to be with you?'

'He is a cook, Sir. He and his large friend.' The sergeant scanned the group looking for Little John and frowned. 'There is another, too, who has a way with horses. They asked us for work and assisted us yesterday.'

'That's it!' shouted the Sheriff in triumph. 'He has a friend who is a big fellow indeed. Now I remember! This young wretch stole my bride from me. He's the boy called Robin Hood. The one who looks after the children of Edwinstowe somewhere in the forest. They make a nuisance of themselves trying to interfere with the good laws of the Sheriff.'

'Edwinstowe!' said the sergeant, realising that he had been fooled.

Robin and Michael had the same thought, then. To make a quick dash for the forest and hope to take the soldiers by surprise. This time, however, the soldiers were not fooled. Before the boys had moved five paces there were a dozen pairs of hands holding them down. Within seconds their hands had been tied behind their backs. They were well and truly prisoners.

'So,' sneered the sergeant, 'our cooks are not everything they seem. Are you going to tell us where the treasure chest is, or do we have to make you tell us?' he roared angrily.

'I will tell you that I am indeed Robin Hood,' said Robin. 'But for that very reason I will not tell you about the treasures which you have taken from the peasants.' He turned to the Sheriff. 'It is you and your men who are the robbers, not us.'

The Sheriff only laughed. 'We'll see how brave you are after a spell in Nottingham Castle,' he said. 'I think you will answer our questions then.'

The rope around the boys' hands was tied to the back of the cart and a company of soldiers was dispatched to accompany them back to Nottingham. Now they did not have the luxury of sitting on the chest in the cart. This time they were forced to run behind, and if they didn't keep up, they would simply be dragged along.

Robin did his best not to appear defeated. The one positive thought he held on to, on that exhausting journey to Nottingham, was the fact that the soldiers had not found the chest. Whatever happened to him, he was determined not to tell, and he was sure that Michael would be equally strong. That way there was the chance that Little John and the other outlaws would be able to go back and cut the chest down. Then at least the villagers would get their precious belongings back.

collecting the treasure

10

William raced back to the camp as fast as his legs would carry him. He charged up to the hidden gate under the fallen tree trunk and banged loudly on the door to be let in.

'Where have you been, William?' asked Friar Tuck as William ran into the camp. 'We were worried about you. Are Robin and Michael far behind you?'

'The sergeant woke up,' panted William. 'So Robin and Michael couldn't get away.' He sank on to the ground, tears running down his face. Marian walked over to him and put her arm round his shoulders.

'Take a deep breath,' she said, 'and then when you are ready, tell us what happened.'

William wiped his face with the back of his hand. 'I hid and watched,' he continued. 'The soldiers searched for the chest for hours and then the Sheriff arrived and recognised Robin. He and Michael are being taken to Nottingham Castle to make them talk. The Sheriff knows they must have had something to do with the theft.'

'What about the treasure chest?' asked Catherine. 'Did they find that?'

'No,' said William. 'It's still hanging in the tree. But who cares about that when Robin and Michael are prisoners in the castle,' he sobbed.

'Nobody owes Robin more that I,' said Marian, speaking to the other children. 'If it hadn't been for his bravery I would have been married to the Sheriff now. I would do anything to free him and Michael, but Robin would want us to fetch the treasure chest.'

'That's certainly true,' said Little John. 'What's more, the Sheriff is not going to give up searching for it. It will only be a matter of time before it is found.'

Everyone was listening to Little John. He was the natural leader when Robin was away. He knew this and took the responsibility seriously.

'I think that we've got to get hold of the chest and bring it back here first of all, although I don't know how because it's so heavy, but we have to find a way. Then we shall have to try and think of a plan to rescue Robin and Michael. Whatever we decide, though, I'm certain it will have a better chance of success by night.'

He looked up at the sun. 'It's still only mid-morning. Today we must get the chest back and while we are doing it, we will try to think of a way of rescuing our friends.'

'How are we going to do that?' asked Friar Tuck. 'Just lifting it up the tree took eight of us and it's two hours' walk from here. We cannot possibly carry it.'

'We could drag it,' said Anna. 'We could tie ropes around it and then pull it.'

'But that would only work if the path was smooth,' said Little John, 'and it is not. It is rough and uneven. The chest would constantly be getting caught in dips and hollows. If we are to drag it, we need a flat, smooth surface to place the chest on.'

As they were talking, Friar Tuck was gazing at the adventure playground that Michael

97

had built. He watched little Mary gliding happily down the long slide made out of a smooth plank of wood. On the other side was a second slide, just the same.

'That's it!' he exclaimed, excitedly. 'We can use Michael's slides! If we fix one on each side of the bottom of the chest it will make it easier to pull along the path.'

Within minutes, Little John and Friar Tuck had cut the slides away from the tree trunk. Catherine agreed to stay in the camp and look after a few of the smaller children while all the rest set off excitedly to the tree where the treasure chest was hidden.

They travelled carefully but quickly. Every so often Little John would insist that they stopped and listened in case there was anyone approaching from behind. The path remained deserted. They didn't see anyone at all.

At last they reached the large old oak tree. Only when they were directly underneath it could they see that the chest was still hanging there, amongst the high branches. There was a murmur of excitement but Little John signalled that everyone must remain quiet. There may be no soldiers here now but there was no telling when they might return.

'Everyone out of the way,' he said. 'I can get the chest down quickly myself.'

There was no time to lower it. Speed was important. Little John climbed the tree and reached the chest in no time. He pulled out his knife and looked down to make sure that everyone was well out of the way. Then he slashed the rope holding the chest in place. After two or three cuts the rope gave way and the chest fell to earth with an almighty crash. The noise was even louder than he had expected, but it was a risk that he had to take.

Everyone stayed hidden for a few moments until they were sure that no one had heard the noise and then they ran forward to look at the chest. Those who had helped to pull it up into the treetop the night before had seen only a dark and distant shape. Now they could see the strong iron plates and the crest which decorated them.

'We shall not waste time breaking the padlock open now,' said Little John, jumping down from the lowest branch of the tree. 'We have tools which will prise that open when we get back to camp.'

So they could only imagine its contents. The gold coins, plates and tankards. The jewellery. And most of all, the sacred golden goblet of Edwinstowe.

Aided by Little John and Friar Tuck, the children lifted first one side of the chest and then the other, while Anna and Marian slipped the slides underneath. Then Little John securely fastened the chest to the slides with the rope. He left a length of rope at the front to pull it along by.

'Now,' said Little John. 'Everyone line up and take hold of the rope. Ready? Pull!'

For a moment nothing happened, then the slides began to move. Everyone smiled. It was very hard work but the chest was moving, although they were only walking at about half normal walking pace. At this rate, Little John reckoned, the return journey would probably take about three times as long as the journey there. Nevertheless, that would still allow then to arrive back in camp before nightfall.

About an hour into the journey, Little

John was about to give the order for a second rest when Anna whispered, urgently.

'Quick, everybody. I hear horses' hooves. Drag the chest into the bushes and hide!'

A close encounter

11

They dragged the chest as far as they could into the bushes and threw a few branches and leaves over it to hide it from view. Then they raced off to find a hiding place. Marian smiled across at Anna, hidden behind a small tree stump. It was remarkable how these children, some as young as seven years old, now acted so quickly and without panicking. Only a few weeks ago they had been just ordinary children and now here they were in the forest helping to rescue stolen treasure. Anna must be very proud of them.

Marian's attention was drawn back to the path where three horsemen were coming round the bend. She gasped as she saw them. These were not soldiers. The man in the centre wore a shirt decorated with a beautiful, brightly-coloured crest. Strapped to the horse was a large iron sword, a helmet and a shield bearing the same crest. Clearly this man was a knight.

The two men who travelled with him wore much more simple clothes. They each had a smaller sword and shield, again decorated with the same crest. There was no knowing what their business was. One thing Marian was sure about was that they would be strong enemies if it came to any form of fight. She prayed that the men would not notice the chest and would pass by without stopping.

At that moment, however, the sun came out from behind a cloud. It shone on the path, the horses and the men. It made their swords and shields flash. And it caught a corner of the iron chest which was not covered by leaves and made it glint brightly.

Marian held her breath, her heart thudding. She hardly dared look. Time seemed to stand still and each moment she expected a shout of discovery.

But none came. The knight and his three companions passed by. When they were well out of sight everyone crept out of the trees. Marian had never seen Little John look so pale. Sweat glistened on his forehead.

No one spoke as they dragged the chest out again and continued on. Whoever the knight was, they could not afford to be caught by anyone.

It was dark when they arrived back at the camp. Everyone was utterly exhausted and pleased to see that Catherine had prepared a simple meal of fish soup and bread. Then the younger ones fell into their beds while the older ones rested in preparation for the rescue attempt that night.

'Has anyone had any ideas about how we can rescue Robin and Michael?' asked Little John, looking round the small group.

They all shook their heads dejectedly.

'Well,' began Friar Tuck. 'It's not much of a plan...'

'Tell us,' said Marian. 'Any plan is better than none.'

'We need an expert with a bow and arrow,' he said. 'And we have that in Catherine.'

Catherine smiled modestly at him.

'We need a long coil of rope,' he continued, pointing to the one which had been round the treasure chest. 'And we need a couple of strong horses, which we don't have.'

'What about the soldiers' horses?' asked Catherine. 'There will be plenty in the stables at the castle.'

Little John was nodding. 'I think I see your plan, Friar Tuck. It's worth a try, but getting enough horses from the stables will be a noisy procedure.'

'Plough horses,' said Marian. 'How many do you have in Edwinstowe?'

'Two,' said Friar Tuck, excitedly. 'And I think they have one in Greenmere which we could borrow.'

Suddenly their tiredness was forgotten and they all smiled at each other. As Catherine had said, any plan was better than none, and now that they had one they couldn't wait to get started.

'God willing,' said Little John, getting to his feet, 'Robin and Michael will be with us before the night is through.'

catherine's arrow

12

'**I** wish Michael was with us,' said Friar Tuck. 'He's so good with horses. I don't know one end of them from the other.'

Little John grinned, tired though he was. It had been a very long day for all of them and it was by no means over yet.

'Those old plough horses won't be any trouble,' he said. 'I'll get the one from Greenmere while you and the others go to Edwinstowe. Seth will help you to harness them. We'll meet at Nottingham Castle.'

At last came the parting of the ways. As Little John left to go into Greenmere he noticed Catherine's worried expression. She knew that the plan depended on her accuracy with the bow and arrow and, although she was known to be the best archer in the camp next to Robin, this was going to be a test indeed. He gave her an encouraging smile and a wave of the hand and left them to continue to Edwinstowe.

It was bright moonlight when they met again in sight of Nottingham Castle. The huge dark building stood out clearly against the surrounding fields and the black water of the moat sparkled brightly.

The little group stood silently for a moment, staring at the seemingly impregnable castle. What did Robin and Michael feel like, locked up in that awful place, and what if everything went wrong and they too found themselves prisoners at the mercy of the Sheriff?

One of the horses stamped and snuffled, which spurred Little John into action. He waved the others forward until they were in the shadow of the castle itself. It was time to put the plan into action.

'How do we even know where they are?' whispered Marian, scanning the sheer walls anxiously. 'They might be in the dungeons. Has anyone thought of that?'

'Pray that they are not,' answered Little John. 'Or our plans will certainly be in vain.'

Motioning them to stay where they were, he crept forward and began to hoot like an owl. Three short hoots, then a pause, then three more.

Nothing happened. There was silence except for the rustling of a small animal in the forest and the three horses moving restlessly.

He tried again. This time there was an answer. Three answering hoots rang out from high above them to the left.

They all grinned at each other and then stared up the vast sheer wall towards where the sound had come from. There was nothing but blackness.

Then Marian saw it. 'There!' she whispered, urgently. 'A tiny glow. They must have lit a candle and put it in the window!'

They could all see it now. A flickering light and two hands waving through the bars of the window. Robin and Michael knew help was at hand.

'They must lie down,' said Catherine. 'I cannot fire an arrow unless I am sure they are expecting it.'

Little John ran out of the shadows and into the moonlight where he could be seen by the two prisoners. Then he stretched out his arms and threw himself to the ground. He got up and did the same thing again.

Catherine gave a little nervous laugh. It was strange to see this giant of a boy falling to the ground in the moonlit field for no obvious reason.

'The hands have gone,' she said. 'They must be lying down now.' She stared up at the square hole with the six bars running from top to bottom. Now was the time for her to shoot the most important arrow of her life.

Just like Robin's arrow in the forest the night before, Catherine's arrow had a long length of rope attached to it. She would have to take this extra weight into account and aim her arrow higher than normal.

Pulling back the bow as far as it would go, she took careful aim. Everyone was silent. Even the horses were still. She hesitated for several seconds, checking her aim. Then she let go of the bow string.

With a soft whooshing sound the arrow flew upwards, the rope snaking behind it. They waited an eternity, necks aching with looking upwards, holding their breaths.

There was a thud as the arrow hit the castle wall, missing its target. Catherine groaned with disappointment and began to pull on the rope, dragging in the arrow to try again.

It had fallen short. She must aim even higher this time.

Determined this time to reach her target, she fitted the arrow into the bowstring for the second time and drew it back. Aim higher, higher, she told herself. Pull. Let it fly.

This time the arrow flew straight in through the square window, missing the bars. Catherine sighed with relief when Little John patted her shoulder in congratulation.

Inside the cell, Robin and Michael lay huddled on the floor. They did not know what to expect but were delighted that their friends had come to attempt to rescue them. At first they didn't know what had happened when the arrow flew into the room. They heard something metallic ping off the wall. Then the arrow fell to the floor and the rope that had trailed behind it fell across their bodies.

Robin was the first to react.

'A rope,' he said. 'It's very clever getting it to us like this, but what are we to do with it? We can't just climb out of the windows since the bars block our way.'

Michael, however, was on his feet and looking down through the window.

'They have three plough horses,' he said. 'I can just see them beyond the moat. Little John is tying the other end of the rope to the horses' harnesses. Help me tie this end to the bars. I believe they're going to pull the bars out.'

Quickly they laced the rope through the six bars. Then Robin gave six hoots to signal that they were ready. Then they watched the horses begin to move forward. After a few yards they stopped as the rope became taut. Little John was urging them forward again, and Robin and Michael could hear the bars creaking under the pressure.

'Come on, don't give up on us now, you horses,' whispered Robin under his breath.

But the bars were obviously well made. They remained securely in place. Then Michael pointed at a section of the rope just beyond the window.

'It's beginning to fray,' he said. 'It's going to snap.'

Then with a sharp crack, one of the bars gave way, then another and another, and they fell out with a clatter and tumbled down into the moat below.

But the noise disturbed a dog which began

barking and soon there were shouts from the soldiers and footsteps on the stone steps outside their cell. They heard the jangle of keys and the rattle as one was fitted into the lock.

'Quick!' said Robin. 'We've got to jump!' He clambered on to the window ledge and launched himself out of the window before he could think about it. Then he was falling through the air for what seemed a very long time.

The ice cold water of the moat knocked the breath out of him and he only dimly heard Michael splash in nearby. Robin was so numb that he could hardly move, it seemed as if he was trying to swim through treacle. Everything looked black and he floundered this way and that until someone called nearby. It was Marian.

'Robin! This way. Here's my hand.'

Robin heard her voice, warm and gentle and swam towards it. Then he felt strong hands grab his arms and drag him out. A blanket was thrown round his shoulders and he was lifted on to one of the horses. He felt it move under him, swiftly, away from the shouting soldiers.

'Quickly!' he heard Little John say. 'The soldiers are running for their horses. It won't be long before they reach us.'

'Michael?' whispered Robin. He felt a hand on his.

'Michael is fine,' said Friar Tuck.

Then there was just the jogging, the dark shapes of the trees as they passed, and Robin dropped off into an exhausted sleep. The next thing he knew he was being pushed under the log which hid their camp from view and willing hands pulled him up the other side.

They were safe!

Robin and Michael felt better when they had changed into dry clothes and had a hot drink. Everyone congratulated Catherine. And in the centre of the clearing the chest full of treasure sparkled in the moonlight. Little John had lost no time in prising open the padlock.

'Where's Friar Tuck?' asked Robin, looking round.

'He was going to hide the horses in a thick part of the forest until the Sheriff's soldiers had gone and then return them to the villages.' said Little John. ' He should be back by dawn.'

Of course, thought Robin. There was no way the horses could get inside the camp. He looked up as Marian came and sat down beside him.

'You've done well, Robin,' she said. 'Your father would be proud of you. It's up to us to do these things while King Richard is away and all the people of the county will be grateful to you – especially when you return their treasures.'

He took her hand. 'Thank you for your part in this, Marian,' he said. 'There is one treasure I would like to waste no time in returning. With all the excitement of the day I find that I am no longer sleepy. Will you come with me Marian? Let us find Friar Tuck and ride with him.'

The next morning when Lizzie walked into the Banquet Hall she was amazed at what she saw. There on the table stood the village's sacred golden goblet, the very same goblet that the Sheriff's men had taken away two

119

days ago. Underneath it she spotted a piece of parchment with words written on it. It simply said:

'We steal from the rich and give to the poor!

Signed, Robin Hood and his outlaws.'